GLITTER

by
Stella J. Jones

Illustrated by
Judi Abbot

tiger tales

There was once a little rhino named Gloria.
And Gloria's favorite color was

glitter!

Which is **silly** because everyone
knows that glitter isn't a real color.
But did Gloria care? **No, she did not!**

Everything in her life
had a little bit of
razzle-dazzle.

She had spanglepants,
glitter slippers,

and a
glitterama-
razzamatazz
scooter!

And everywhere Gloria went, she left a little bit of glittery happiness behind her.

Just

like

this.

She **glittered** the banker,

the barber, the baker.

She **dazzled** the chef

and the cabinet-maker.

She **glitzed** up the plumbers,

she **spangled** the drummers,

she **spritzed up** the teachers and the long-distance runners.

Don't they look **glorious**?!

Don't they look **happy**?!

Actually,
they don't look very happy, do they?
This is awkward.

"No more glitter, Gloria!"
they all told the little rhino.
But did Gloria hear them? No, she did not!

There was only one thing to do –
scrub that glitter off!

But (as everyone knows) once
glorious glitter is used,

it goes everywhere!

uh-oh.

SPOILER ALERT

It's about to get **messy**!

Wally the lion
bumped
into Fred,

who **ran** into

Maisy and Daisy—
how crazy!

Then Harry **hugged** Larry,

who **shook paws** with Gary

who **high-fived** and **fist-bumped** both Sally and Barry!

Soon Gloria's glitter had covered
the **entire town!**

There was some on the **tower**
and **lots** on the **steeple,**
As well as the **market**
and all of the **people.**

Even Pa Elephant,
on his way to see
Skunk . . .

. . . got patches of **glitter**
all over **his trunk!**

Oh, no! Everyone was so grumpy before.
Will they be **really angry** now?

What will they say?
What will they do?

But instead of **Shouting** and **Stomping** and **Snorting** . . . there was **smiling, giggling, chuckling,** and **chortling!**

Just like the glitter that was spread all around,
the **happiness** traveled right through the town!

Phew! Everyone loves a happy ending!

Hooray for Gloria!

She made the town smile with her
razzle-dazzle!

And even though it's clear to see that glitter STILL
isn't really a color, did Gloria care?

No, she did not!

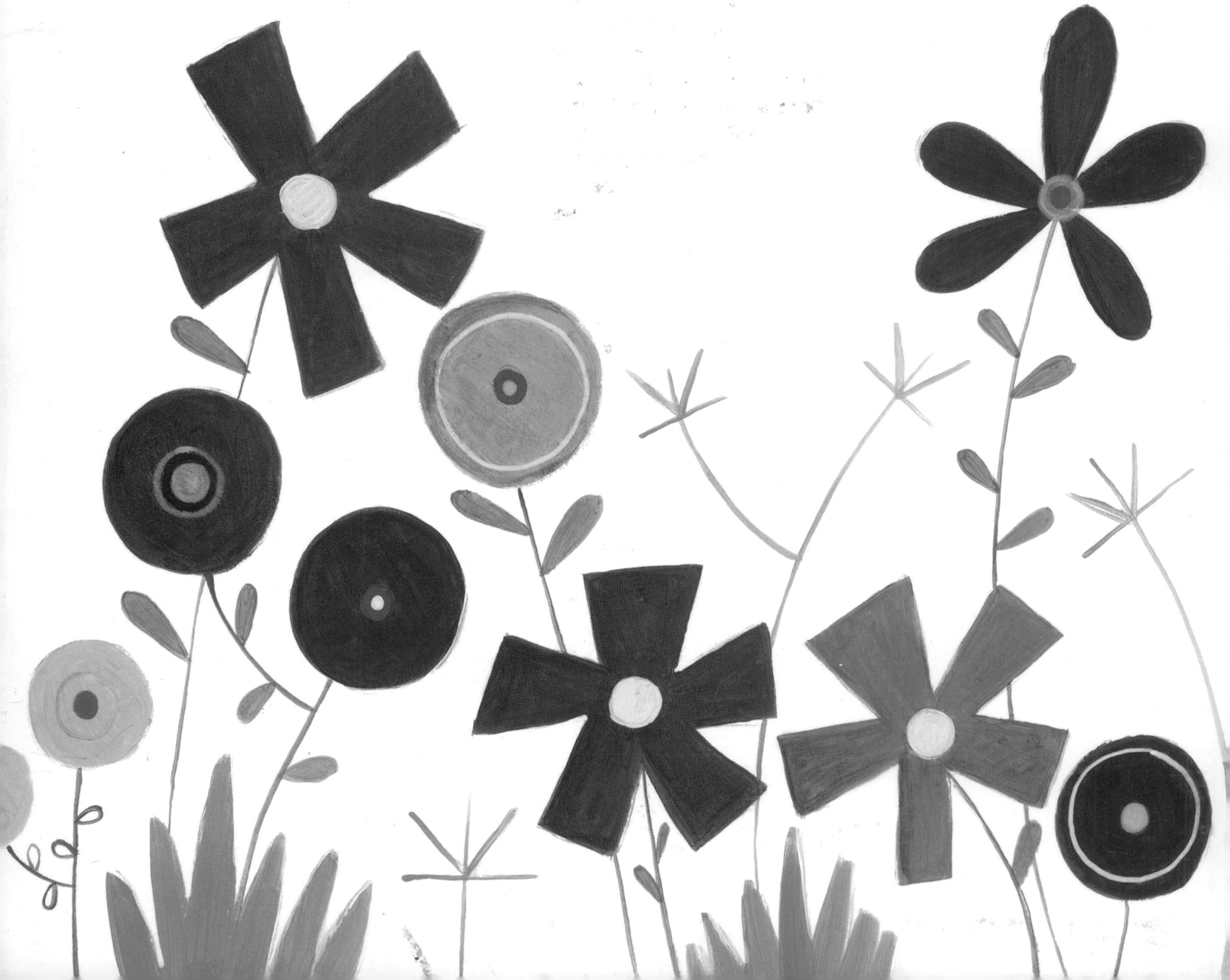